by Jayneen Sanders   illustrated by Farimah Khavarinezhad

BODY SAFETY RED FLAGS

Educating children about body safety, consent, and the
subtle red flags that may indicate grooming, both online and offline

Body Safety Red Flags
Educate2Empower Publishing an imprint of
UpLoad Publishing Pty Ltd
Victoria Australia
www.upload.com.au

This edition first published in 2024
Text copyright © Jayneen Sanders 2024
Illustration copyright © UpLoad Publishing Pty Ltd 2024

Written by Jayneen Sanders
Illustrations by Farimah Khavarinezhad

Jayneen Sanders asserts her right to be identified as the author of this work.
Farimah Khavarinezhad asserts her right to be identified as the illustrator of this work.

Designed by Stephanie Spartels, Studio Spartels

Printed in China through Book Production Solutions

ISBN: 9781761160493 (hbk) 9781761160486 (pbk)

A catalogue record for this
book is available from the
National Library of Australia

Thank you to Professor Kerryann Walsh and the team at Queensland University of
Technology for their invaluable suggestions and edits re the content of this book.

Disclaimer: The information in this book is advice only written by the author based on her advocacy in this area, and her experience working with children as a classroom teacher and mother. The information is not meant to be a substitute for professional services or advice. For professional help if you are concerned about a child's behavior, go to a health professional and/or contact the key organizations listed at www.e2epublishing.info

Notes to Parents, Caregivers, and Educators

Thank you so much for taking the time to read this book with your child. 'Body Safety Red Flags' should be read and unpacked over a number of sessions. Note: please ensure if your child does use a device such as a tablet, phone or computer, they do not use it in a private space such as a bedroom or bathroom. Devices should only be used in a public space.

With approximately 1 in 9 girls and 1 in 20 boys experiencing sexual abuse before 18[1] and with 90% of the offenders known to the child[2] (see page 39 for sources), it is well and truly time to unpack grooming behaviors, both online and offline.

This book, 'Body Safety Red Flags':
- uses empowering scenarios to educate children about what to do in situations where they feel unsafe or unsure. Written and illustrated in an age-appropriate and child-friendly way, this book draws attention to the subtle grooming techniques that offenders may use to groom children.

- is written in a way that empowers children and builds their confidence. It does not use fear-based or scare tactics; which, in fact, have been proven to be ineffective.

- educates adults about the subtle grooming techniques offenders may use; keeping in mind that offenders can 'groom' children and the adults around them.

Offenders, whether known to the child or first met online, often use the digital space to groom children. In daily life, offenders appear as the friendliest, nicest, most helpful people in the world, and this performance is quite deliberate. They will work very hard to gain your trust so that if your child does disclose inappropriate behavior by them, it will be very hard to believe what you are hearing.

See 'Grooming Red Flags Checklist' poster.
Please share this checklist with family, friends and
your community. Free to download from:
www.e2epublishing.info

Hi! I'm Darby!

In stories and in real life, a **red flag** means there may be danger ahead.

A red flag gives us a warning.

It tells us something is NOT safe.

In this book, you will learn many body safety skills to help keep you safe, and how to recognize body safety red flags.

Your body is very smart. When it feels unsafe it will let you know. You might get a sick feeling in your tummy or your heart might beat really fast. These feelings are called your **Early Warning Signs**. Your Early Warning Signs are a red flag.

If you feel unsafe, you might feel just one or two of your Early Warning Signs, or you might feel many Early Warning Signs like Stevie in the picture below.

IF I FEEL **UNSAFE** MY BODY LETS ME KNOW.

SWEATY BROW

HAIR FEELS LIKE IT IS STANDING ON END

STARTS TO CRY

GOOSEBUMPS

HEART BEATS FAST

SHAKY ALL OVER

FEELS SICK IN THE TUMMY

SWEATY PALMS

NEEDS TO GO TO THE TOILET

WOBBLY LEGS

WHICH EARLY WARNING SIGNS HAVE YOU FELT AND WHEN?

If a person makes you feel unsafe, they may be a 'tricky' person.

🚩 A 'tricky' person is someone who might make you feel uncomfortable or unsafe.

🚩 They might not listen to you when you say 'Stop!' or when you say, 'I don't like that!'

🚩 They may ask you to keep secrets from your safe adults.

🚩 They might want you to share pictures or information about yourself online or chat to you more than you are allowed.

🚩 And they may not respect your *body boundary.

*Your body boundary is the invisible space around your body. It's your personal space — a space just for you. People need to ask for your consent before entering your body boundary. Everyone has a body boundary — adults, teenagers, children and babies.

Note to adult: to further unpack the meaning of consent go to page 19.

Q: If ever you feel unsafe, do you know what to do?

A: That's right! You need to tell a safe and *__trusted__ adult on your *__Safety Network__ as soon as you can. They will listen to you and they will know how to help you.

*A safe and trusted adult is a grown-up who:
- cares for you very much
- makes you feel safe
- always listens to you
- respects your voice and your body boundary
- will always believe you when you say you are feeling uncomfortable, worried or unsafe
- will be able to help you.

*A Safety Network is 3 to 5 safe adults that you trust. These are the people who, if you told them anything that made you feel worried or unsafe, would listen to you, believe you and know how to help you. One adult on your Safety Network should not be in your family. If you want to learn how to make your own Safety Network Hand, go to page 33.

DARBY'S SAFETY NETWORK

MAMA

DAD

MS LING (TEACHER)

GRANDMA

→ WHO ARE THE PEOPLE ON YOUR SAFETY NETWORK?

Sometimes I like tickling games ...

... and sometimes I don't. Sometimes I feel my Early Warning Signs and I don't want to be tickled anymore.

So, when I say 'Stop!' the person who is tickling me needs to stop.

If they don't stop, I need to tell a trusted adult on my Safety Network as soon as I can.

Tickling me when I say 'Stop!' is NOT okay!

REMEMBER!

IF ONE OF YOUR SAFE ADULTS IS NOT AROUND OR DOES NOT LISTEN TO YOU AND HELP YOU, KEEP TELLING OTHER SAFE ADULTS ON YOUR SAFETY NETWORK UNTIL YOU ARE HELPED.

DO YOU LIKE TICKLING GAMES?
DO PEOPLE LISTEN TO YOU
WHEN YOU SAY 'STOP!'?

If someone tickles you or touches your body in a way that makes you feel uncomfortable or unsafe, like touching or tickling your *private parts, this is NOT okay!

*Your private parts are the parts of your body under your bathing suit or underwear. Both adults and children need to use the correct names for their private parts. Boys usually have a penis, testicles and a bottom. Girls usually have a vulva on the outside and a vagina on the inside. They also have nipples and a bottom. When girls get older, the area around their nipples grows into breasts. A person's bottom is also known as their buttocks. Your mouth is a private part too. And even though it can be seen, it is still private. (Private means just for you.)

Q: If you are touched in an unsafe way, what do you need to do?

A: That's right! You need to tell a trusted adult on your Safety Network as soon as you can.

Tickling or touching your private parts is NOT okay!

If an older person spends lots of time just with you, and says you are way more special than other children, or buys you lots of presents or gives you lots of treats, this might be a red flag.

If they tell you not to tell anyone or ask you to keep secrets, this is NOT okay!

🚩 And if you are talking to a person online, and they tell you that you are very very special or ask you to meet offline, this is NOT okay!

🚩 It is also NOT okay if they try to trick you into doing things you don't want to do by buying you things or offering you game coins or gifts.

🚩 These things are especially NOT okay if they tell you not to tell your trusted adults and to keep the chats secret.

Q: If any of these things happen, what do you need to do?

A: That's right! You need to tell a trusted adult on your Safety Network as soon as you can.

REMEMBER!

SOMETIMES A PERSON MIGHT TELL YOU NOT TO TELL AN UNSAFE SECRET, AND YOU MIGHT FEEL TOO SCARED TO TELL SOMEONE ON YOUR SAFETY NETWORK. BUT ALWAYS REMEMBER, IT IS NEVER TOO LATE TO TELL A SAFE ADULT WHAT HAS HAPPENED.

If someone tells you to keep a **secret** — especially if they say not to tell any of your trusted adults, you can say, 'I don't keep secrets — only happy **surprises** because they will always be told.'

Telling kids to keep a secret is NOT okay!

Q: If this happens, what do you need to do?

A: That's right! You need to tell a trusted adult on your Safety Network as soon as you can.

→ HAS ANYONE ASKED YOU TO KEEP A SECRET?

If someone tries to hug or kiss you or enter your body boundary without your *consent, this is NOT okay! They are not respecting your personal body boundary.

Q: If this happens, what do you need to do?

A: That's right! You need to tell a trusted adult on your Safety Network as soon as you can.

MAY I HAVE A HUG?

YES!

*Consent is an important word. It means asking if something is okay or not okay. It means one person asks for permission and another person gives permission or they don't. One person asks if it is okay, and the other person says if it is okay or not.

→ DO PEOPLE ASK FOR YOUR CONSENT BEFORE THEY KISS OR HUG YOU?

Private means just for you. A private space is your bedroom, the bathroom and the toilet. No one should enter your private space without knocking, and asking you if it's okay for them to come in.

If they don't knock first, this is NOT okay!

Q: If someone does not respect your private space, what do you need to do?

A: That's right! You need to tell a trusted adult on your Safety Network as soon as you can.

WHAT ARE THE PRIVATE SPACES IN YOUR HOUSE?

WHAT ARE THE PUBLIC SPACES (WHERE EVERYONE CAN GO) IN YOUR HOUSE?

If a person asks you (or takes you) to spend alone time just with them in a space where others can't see like a bedroom, bathroom or in a playhouse, this is NOT okay!

This is especially NOT okay if they tell you to keep it a secret.

And if you are playing a game online
and someone asks you to go to a
private chat, this is also NOT okay.

Q: If any of these things happen, what do you need to do?

A: That's right! You need to tell a trusted adult on your
Safety Network as soon as you can.

If someone asks you to play computer or video games with them, and asks you for personal information (like your birthday, phone number or school name) or gives you game coins or gifts, this is NOT okay!

This is also NOT okay if they ask you to keep it a secret.

Q: If this happens, what do you need to do?

A: That's right! You need to tell a trusted adult on your Safety Network as soon as you can.

REMEMBER!
ALWAYS CHECK IN WITH ONE OF YOUR SAFE ADULTS FIRST BEFORE YOU PLAY ANY COMPUTER GAMES WITH ANYONE.

HAS ANYONE ASKED YOU TO PLAY COMPUTER OR VIDEO GAMES WITHOUT A SAFE ADULT KNOWING?

If someone touches your private parts, asks you to touch or look at their private parts or shows you pictures of private parts, this is NOT okay!

Q: If this happens, what do you need to do?

A: That's right! You need to tell a trusted adult on your Safety Network as soon as you can.

If someone asks you to take pictures of your private parts and share them on a phone, a tablet, or a computer, or sends photos of their private parts to you, this is NOT okay!

Q: If this happens, what do you need to do?

A: That's right! You need to tell a trusted adult on your Safety Network as soon as you can.

And if someone 'chats' to you online and the conversation makes you feel uncomfortable or unsafe, this is NOT okay!

It is especially NOT okay if they:

- tell you not to tell anyone about your 'chats'
- ask you to join a private chat without your safe adult knowing
- ask you to keep online things secret
- ask to meet you offline.

Q: If any of these things happen, what do you need to do?

A: That's right! You need to tell a trusted adult on your Safety Network as soon as you can.

REMEMBER!

A safe adult will always **respect** your body boundary and will always ask before they hug or kiss you. They will ask for your **consent**.

A safe adult will stop as soon as you say, 'No' or 'Stop' to tickling or hugs or someone entering your body boundary.

A safe person will speak kindly to kids in games and only talk about the games – not unsafe things. They will also ask one of the people on your Safety Network if they can play a game with you.

A safe adult will listen to you, believe you and help you when you feel unsafe.

REMEMBER!

You are never to blame if a person has tricked you or made you feel unsafe. You will NOT get into trouble if you tell a safe adult.

BODY SAFETY WORDS TO KNOW

Body Boundary: the invisible personal space around your body (this includes assistive devices such as a wheelchair)

Consent: asking if something is okay or not okay; asking for and giving permission; saying or showing an enthusiastic 'yes' or saying or showing 'no'

Early Warning Signs: the physical things that happen to our body when we are worried, uncomfortable, scared or unsafe

Private: a space or a body part that is just for you

Public: a space everyone uses, for example, the kitchen

Respect: understanding another person's wishes, treating them the way you want to be treated, and caring about them and their wishes

Safety Network: 3 to 5 safe and trusted adults that you could go to if you feel scared or worried or unsafe, and they will listen, believe you and help you

Secrets: information that is often kept from others and may never be told

Surprises: information that is most often happy and will always be told

Tricky Person: someone who makes you feel unsafe and/or uncomfortable; they do not listen to your voice and/or they do not respect your body boundary, they may ask you to keep secrets that make you feel uncomfortable

Trust: belief in a person who wants the best for you and cares for you, and would never harm you

MAKE A SAFETY NETWORK HAND

You will need:

- a piece of paper
- colored pencils
- a trusted adult

1. Spread your hand out on the paper.

2. Have your adult draw around your hand.

3. Choose 3 to 5 safe and trusted adults to be on your Safety Network (one should not be a family member).

4. Write each adult's name on a finger. If you can't write just yet, have your adult write the names and you draw their pictures.

MAMA
DAD
MS LING
GRANDMA

DARBY'S SAFETY NETWORK

Note to adult: these safe and trusted adults are to be your child's choice, and they should be accessible and notified of this honor!

KEY BODY SAFETY PHRASES

MY BODY BELONGS TO ME!

I AM THE BOSS OF MY BODY!

THIS IS MY BODY! WHAT I SAY GOES!

I HAVE A VOICE AND I CAN USE IT.

I CAN SAY 'NO' TO HUGS AND KISSES. I CAN CHOOSE HOW I GREET PEOPLE.

I DON'T KEEP SECRETS — ONLY HAPPY SURPRISES BECAUSE THEY WILL ALWAYS BE TOLD.

PEOPLE NEED TO ASK FOR MY CONSENT BEFORE ENTERING MY BODY BOUNDARY.

PEOPLE NEED TO RESPECT MY WISHES. SO, WHEN I SAY 'NO', I MEAN 'NO'.

I CAN SAY 'NO' TO TICKLES AND TOUCHES.

I CALL MY PRIVATE PARTS BY THEIR CORRECT NAMES.

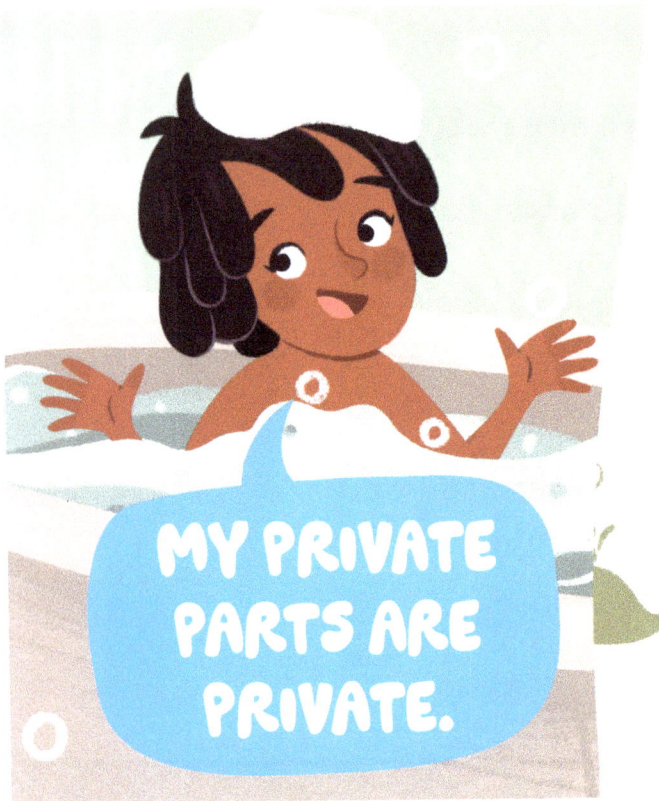

MY PRIVATE PARTS ARE PRIVATE.

IF I FEEL UNSAFE, I CAN TELL A TRUSTED ADULT ON MY SAFETY NETWORK.

DISCUSSION QUESTIONS
for Parents, Caregivers, and Educators

The following Discussion Questions are intended as a guide and can be used to initiate open and empowering conversations with your child around the subtle grooming red flags an adult or another child may use, as well as what to do if they feel unsafe – the default, even if they fear the offender, is to tell a trusted adult on their Safety Network as soon as they can.

The questions below are optional and/or can be explored at different readings. I suggest you allow your child time to answer the questions both on the internal pages and in this section, as well as encourage them to ask their own questions around this very important topic. It is equally important that you value their input and listen to their voice. All of these discussions will help increase your child's skills and knowledge around personal body safety and consent, and will boost their confidence and empowerment. Remain calm and confident discussing this topic with your child as they will take their cues from you. Praise your child's responses and let them know you will always listen; no matter what.

If there is a disclosure, stay calm – as your initial reaction is key to the child's ongoing health and healing. Reassure the child that:

- you believe them
- they have done the right thing in telling you
- they are incredibly brave and courageous
- they are in no way to blame
- they are safe and will be looked after
- you will do everything you can to stop the abuse, but make no promises.

Leave the child with a trusted adult and contact a sexual assault organization in your local area. There is also a list of organizations in 'Body Safety Education' or on the Educate2Empower website (www.e2epublishing.info). Do not handle a disclosure on your own.

· ·

Pages 4-5

Introduce Darby. Note: your child may know Darby from the children's book *My Body! What I Say Goes!* as a friend of the main character in that book, Stevie. Unpack the meaning of a red flag and where we may see it in 'real life'. Explain that in this book, when they see the red flag, it means a situation is unsafe and they will need to tell a trusted and safe adult. Discuss the two large images. Ask, 'Why is Darby thinking "red flag" as she swims? What do you think the boy is whispering to Darby? Why might she look worried at what he is saying?'

Page 6

After reading page 6, ask, 'What Early Warning Signs have you had? Where were you when these happened?' Discuss how sometimes when we do something exciting, like going down a big water slide, we might also get some of these signs. However, explain we also get them when we are in an unsafe situation or with a person who makes us feel unsafe. Ask, 'What should you do if you get some of your Early Warning Signs and you feel unsafe?' Say, 'That's right! Tell a trusted adult who makes you feel safe.'

Page 7

Use the term 'tricky people' to explain people who make a child feel unsafe. Tricky people are not just strangers, they can be people your child knows who may be in their family or community. Go through the list on page 7 with your child. Unpack each point and explain that these are red flags – they give us a warning that something is not right. **Note:** ensure your child knows what the terms 'online' and 'offline' mean. Reinforce that when we get a red flag, we need to tell a safe and trusted adult as soon as possible. Talk about a body boundary and together outline your invisible body boundaries. Consent can be unpacked here or on page 19.

Pages 8-9

Discuss what the words 'safe' and 'trusted' mean. Introduce your child to a Safety Network. Unpack each point on page 8. Help your child develop their own Safety Network by exploring page 33. **Note:** this could be done at another time or while reading this section.

Pages 10-11

Note: 'tickling' can be used as a grooming technique where the offender does not listen to the child when they say 'Stop!' or accidentally/on-purpose tickles the child's private parts to desensitize them to being touched intimately. Reinforce to your child to keep telling until they are believed and helped. Also, this might be a good time to let other family members know that if your child says 'Stop!' to tickling or being touched in any way, they must stop immediately. Ask, 'Have you ever had any of your Early Warning Signs when someone was tickling you?' If they answer 'Yes', ask them if they can explain a little more about what happened.

Pages 12-13

Now might be a good time to explain what 'private' and 'public' means in relation to body parts. Reiterate that 'private' means just for you, and that no one should touch or tickle their private parts. Reinforce the message that if this happens, they need to tell a trusted adult on their Safety Network. Ask, 'Who do you think Darby is telling?' **Note:** your child's mouth is also a private part, as are boys' nipples. Explain to your child that even though a boy's nipples are private they are not covered by a bathing suit or underwear. At this time, you may also like to introduce the word 'public'. Talk about our 'public' body parts as those that we all see such as our ears, nose and arms (but not the mouth). You could also relate 'private' and 'public' to places such as a toilet being a private place and a kitchen being a public place. Reassure your child that it is okay for them to touch their own private parts (as it can feel good) but only in a private place such as their own bedroom. If you wish to show your child appropriate drawings of private parts to discuss the difference between genders anatomically, you can download free age-appropriate line drawings of children's private parts at *www.e2epublishing.info* (search for 'Body Parts Activity').

Pages 14-15

We know, those whose intention is to sexually abuse children, will groom both the family and the child. They will make the child feel very special and give them more attention than other children. It is particularly dangerous for children in the online space. **Note:** ensure your child knows what the terms 'online' and 'offline' mean. Offenders may use 'chats' to tell the child that they are very special, that they understand them while others do not; they may buy them gifts and game coins, and ask for personal information. **Note:** if a child is in an online private chat with an uncle, for example, this is only okay if one of their safe adults knows about it. Take your time to unpack each of the five red flags. There are more online red flags discussed on pages 24 to 29. Reinforce with your child that they are never to blame for other's unsafe behaviors, and it is never too late to tell a trusted adult.

Pages 16-17

Reinforce the difference between secrets and surprises, i.e. secrets can make us feel bad and uncomfortable, and can be kept for a very long time; whereas surprises will be told and are kept only for a short length of time. Ask, 'What is a surprise you have kept? Why was it a surprise and not a secret?' **Note:** if your child wishes to share something with you that they don't want others to know about, this is called a 'private conversation' rather than a secret.

Pages 18-19

Unpack the meaning of 'consent'. Reinforce that only an enthusiastic 'Yes!' is consent. Statements such as 'No', 'I'm not sure', 'Nup', 'I don't want to', etc. mean no consent has been given. Silence means 'No' also. Point out that consent can also be withdrawn at any time. Ask, 'How is Darby feeling about the hug from the woman on page 18? Why do you say that?' Discuss that doctors, dentists, nurses and other healthcare professionals need to ask for consent before entering a person's body boundary. See the books *Let's Talk About Body Boundaries, Consent & Respect* and *My Body! What I Say Goes!* by Jayneen Sanders for more in-depth conversations around body boundaries and consent.

Pages 20-21

Review private and public spaces in your house, school and community.

Pages 22-23

People who abuse children aim to get them alone; isolating them so others can't see the abuse. Therefore, ensure your child knows that they should not go to a place with another person where they will not be seen by others. It is very important that you know at all times who your child is chatting to privately online. Ask, 'Has anyone asked you to chat privately online? Who was that person? Please tell me a bit more.'

Pages 24-25

If your child is using a tablet, phone or computer they can be targeted by sexual offenders. Note: these devices should never be used by your child in a private space such as a bedroom, bathroom or toilet. Research tells us that sexual images are most often taken and sent from private spaces. Ensure you go over the points on pages 24 to 25 carefully with your child. Ask, 'Has anyone asked you to share personal information online or offline?' Also ask the question at the base of page 25, and if your child says 'Yes', ask them to explain further.

Pages 26-27

Reiterate to your child that no one should touch their private parts. However, if they are sick or need some kind of medical assistance, then as long as the doctor asks for consent, and you or a trusted adult from their Safety Network is in the room, this may be permissible.

Pages 28-29

Read these pages with your child and ask if they have any questions. Ask, 'Have any of these things happened to you?' If they say 'Yes' ask them to explain further. Reinforce that they will not get into trouble if any of these things have happened, but it is very important that they tell you what has occurred. Note: over recent years, child-on-child sexual abuse has become more common. Ensure your child knows that no one should touch their private parts or ask to view their private parts – even if that person is another child or sibling.

Pages 30-31

Read these pages with your child and ask if they have any questions. Reiterate to your child that they are never to blame if someone has tricked them or made them feel unsafe.

Pages 32-33

Review these terms. Make a Safety Network with your child to display in a prominent place.

Pages 34-36

Practice these empowering phrases with your child.

Sources
1. Finklehor, D. & Shattuck, A. Heather, A. Turner, & Sherry L. Hamby, *The Lifetime Prevalence of Child Sexual Abuse and Sexual Assault Assessed in Late Adolescence*, 55 Journal of Adolescent Health 329, 329-333 (2014).

2. Finklehor, D. & Shattuck, A. (2012) *Characteristics of crimes against juveniles*, Durham, NH: Crimes Against Children Research Centre.

BOOKS BY THE SAME AUTHOR

Body Safety Education
A parents' guide to protecting kids from sexual abuse

This essential and easy-to-read guide contains simple, practical, and age-appropriate ideas on how parents, caregivers and educators can protect children from sexual abuse — ensuring they grow up as assertive and confident teenagers and adults.

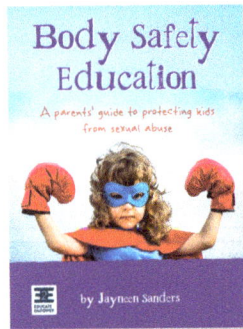

No Means No!

'No Means No!' is a children's picture book about an empowered little girl who has a very strong and clear voice in all issues, especially those relating to her body. This book teaches children about personal boundaries, respect, and consent; empowering kids by respecting their choices and their right to say, 'No!' Discussion Questions included. Suitable for children 2 to 9 years.

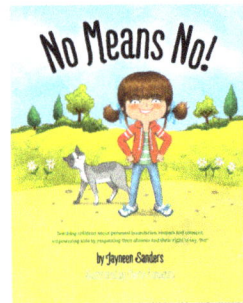

ABC of Body Safety and Consent

The 26 'key' letters and accompanying words and illustrations will help children to learn and consolidate crucial and life-changing body safety and consent skills. Discussion Questions included. Suitable for children 4 to 10 years.

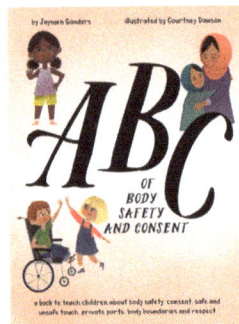

Some Secrets Should Never Be Kept

'Some Secrets Should Never Be Kept' is an award-winning and beautifully illustrated children's book that sensitively raises the subject of inappropriate touch. This book was written as a tool to help parents, caregivers, and teachers broach the subject with children in an age-appropriate and non-threatening way. Discussion Questions included. Suitable for children 3 to 11 years.

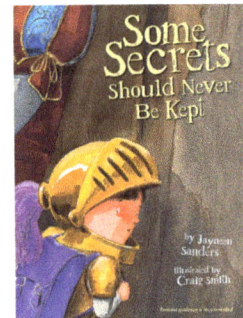

My Body! What I Say Goes!

A children's picture book to empower and teach children about personal body safety, feelings, safe and unsafe touch, private parts, secrets and surprises, consent and respect. Discussion Questions included. Suitable for children 3 to 9 years.

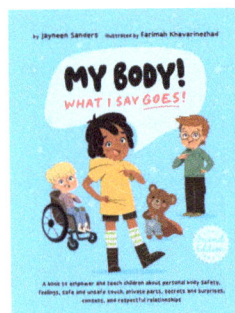

Let's Talk About Body Boundaries, Consent and Respect

Through familiar scenarios, this book opens up crucial conversations with children around consent and respect. A child growing up knowing they have a right to their own personal space, gives that child ownership and choices as to what happens to them. These concepts are presented in a child-friendly and easily-understood manner. Discussion Questions included. Suitable for children 4 to 10 years.

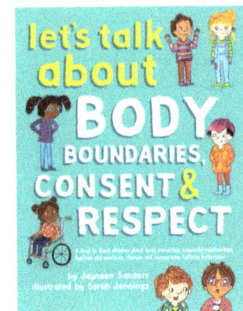

My Body Safety Rules

A children's picture book to educate and empower children with disability about body boundaries, consent and body safety skills. Discussion Questions included. Suitable for children 5+ years.

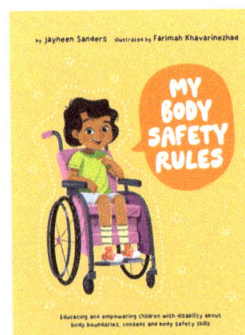

for more books and free resources go to www.e2epublishing.info

www.ingramcontent.com/pod-product-compliance
Lightning Source LLC
Chambersburg PA
CBHW041635040426
42448CB00021B/3485